SECRET PAL
SURPRISES

SECRET PAL SURPRISES

Suzanne Williams

ILLUSTRATED BY Jackie Snider

Hyperion Paperbacks for Children
NEW YORK

For my nieces and nephews:
Crystal, Vikki, Brianna, Sami, Becky,
Mike, Lindsay, Alex, David,
and Karen
—S. W.

First Hyperion Paperback Edition

Text © 1999 by Suzanne Williams.
Illustrations © 1999 by Jackie Snider.

Printed in the United States of America.

First Edition

3 5 7 9 10 8 6 4 2

The artwork for this book is prepared using pencil.
The text for this book is set in 16-point Berkeley Book.

Library of Congress Cataloging-in-Publication Data

Williams, Suzanne.
Secret pal surprises / Suzanne Williams ; illustrated by Jackie Snider.
p.   cm. — (Hyperion chapters)
Summary: Jake, a new big kid in Tommy's third grade class, is Tommy's secret Valentine's Day pal, but Tommy suspects that instead of giving presents Jake is taking things from other students.
ISBN 0-7868-1219-2 (pbk.) — ISBN 0-7868-2270-8 (lib. bdg.)
[1. Stealing—Fiction. 2. Schools—Fiction. 3. Valentine's Day—Fiction.
4. Conduct of life—Fiction.]
I. Snider Jackie, ill. II. Title. III. Series.
PZ7.W66824Se   1998
[Fic]—dc21   97-51955

Contents

1

The Turtle

Tommy Chen looked up from his desk. Mrs. Hall was busy at the blackboard. Tommy took a deep breath. It was now or never. He tucked his glue bottle under his sweatshirt and crept toward the table at the back of the room, behind the coatracks.

The table was covered with little clay animals. Tommy spotted the turtle between a painted pink pig with a lumpy snout and a brown thing that could have been a dog. Or a horse. It was hard to tell.

He picked up the turtle. Two of its legs stayed behind on the table. Tommy slipped

the glue bottle out from under his sweat-shirt. He squirted glue onto one of the turtle's legs and held it against the turtle's body. A little of the glue oozed out, making his fingers sticky.

Tommy hadn't meant to break the turtle. It was an accident. He'd been looking at it earlier that morning when its legs just fell off. Of course, he had bumped the turtle a teensy bit when it attack-landed on the rhino. At least the rhino was okay.

The bad part was, the turtle wasn't his. He had made a snake. But even though his third grade teacher, Mrs. Hall, had warned everyone not to, he rolled it too thin. The snake cracked into a zillion pieces when it dried.

As he glued on the second leg, Tommy wondered whom the turtle belonged to.

Suddenly, he heard footsteps.

Setting the turtle down, Tommy stepped to one side of the coatrack, then looked back at the table. He gulped. His glue was in plain sight. And his name was on the bottle! The footsteps came closer. Tommy

jerked his head back from the edge of the coatrack just as Jake came around the other side.

Jake was new to Fair Ridge Elementary, and he was big. So big he could've passed for a fifth grader. His jeans jacket was too small for him. It stretched tight across his back and the sleeves were too short for his arms. Even so, the jacket would be huge on Tommy.

Hugging the side of the coatrack, Tommy tried hard not to breathe. He hoped Jake wouldn't notice the glue. He hoped Jake wouldn't notice him. What if the turtle belonged to Jake? He could get awfully mad sometimes.

A rustling sound caught Tommy's ear. What was Jake up to? Carefully, Tommy peeked around the edge of the coatrack, and right into Jake's startled face.

2

Valentine Hearts and Secret Pals

Jake shoved something behind a coat. "What are you doing here?" he growled when he saw Tommy.

"I-I was looking for something." Tommy snatched his glue bottle off the table and hurried back to his desk.

As he plopped into his seat, Elizabeth, who sat across from him, looked up. "Are you okay?" she asked. "You look sick or something."

"I'm fine." Tommy watched Elizabeth's

legs swinging back and forth under her chair. She was so short her feet didn't touch the floor.

Jennifer, who sat in back of him, tapped him on the shoulder. "Maybe you should go to the nurse's office," she said.

Tommy rolled his eyes. Jennifer spent more time in the nurse's room than any other kid in the class. She always had a sore throat, or a stomachache. At least she pretended to, anyway.

"I'm fine," he said again. He opened his math book so they would leave him alone.

During art period, everyone worked on their valentine mailboxes. "Try to finish up today," Mrs. Hall said, stapling fat red hearts on the bulletin board. "Valentine's Day is only a week away."

Tommy sneaked a look at Jake, two seats behind him. Jake was bent over his desk, squeezing a glop of glue onto a wet, wrinkled heart. Suddenly, he crumpled up the heart, and threw it onto the floor. Glancing up, he saw Tommy watching him. "Valentine's Day is stupid," Jake muttered. He kicked the crumpled heart across the room.

Tommy hoped Jake would forget about seeing him at the coatracks.

At the end of the day Mrs. Hall held up a basket. "We're going to draw names for secret pals." Her dangly earrings jiggled as she talked. "You can leave little gifts for your secret pal all next week." Mrs. Hall smiled. "Be sneaky though. Don't let your secret pal find out who you are. Not until the Valentine's Day party on Friday, that is."

She stopped at Tommy's desk. Tommy reached into the basket and pulled out a paper slip. His heart sank. Jake! What rotten luck! Anybody's name would have been better than Jake's, even a girl's.

"Remember to take your clay animals home today," Mrs. Hall said after everyone had drawn names.

Tommy wished his snake had made it.

When Elizabeth came back from the clay table, the turtle was cupped in her hands. The turtle was hers! Tommy hoped the glue would hold.

As the class rushed out to the buses, Tommy tripped. He sprawled onto the cement, skinning his knee.

A hand reached out to help him up.

Tommy grabbed it, without looking to see whose it was.

"Better watch where you're going," Jake said gruffly, hauling Tommy to his feet.

Tommy dropped Jake's hand. He'd heard that Jake sometimes tripped other kids. Maybe it hadn't been an accident.

"Listen," Jake said, tugging at the collar of his too-small jacket. "Don't tell Mrs. Hall you saw me. Okay? At the coatracks, I mean."

"Okay," said Tommy. He wouldn't want to do anything that would make Jake mad at him. No telling what Jake might do.

3

The Balloon

On Monday morning Tommy opened his pencil box and found a wrinkled balloon taped to the top of his case. A note next to the balloon said, "From your secret pal." Tommy fingered the balloon. It was black with white stars. He could hardly wait to blow it up.

"Look what my secret pal gave me," he said to Elizabeth.

"It's pretty," she said, swinging her legs back and forth. "You must have a nice secret pal."

Tommy nodded. Then he remembered the clay turtle, how it belonged to Elizabeth. He wondered if its legs were still glued on. "How's your turtle?" The words just slipped out.

"My turtle?" Elizabeth looked confused. "He died," she said. "He's dead."

Tommy gulped.

"It happened two weeks ago," Elizabeth said. "So I made a clay turtle. To remember him by."

Phew! Looking down at his desk, Tommy asked, "Is the clay turtle okay?"

"Of course," Elizabeth said, sounding surprised. "Why wouldn't it be?"

Tommy shrugged. "No reason."

Jake walked by on his way back from the pencil sharpener. "Nice balloon," he said, leaning over Tommy's desk. "Where did you get it?"

"From my secret pal," Tommy said. He wished Jake wouldn't stand so close.

"Can I see it?" Jake asked.

Reluctantly, Tommy handed Jake the balloon.

He stretched it this way and that.

"Careful," Tommy said. "You'll rip a hole in it."

"No, I won't." Finally, Jake handed the balloon back. Tommy slipped it into his pants pocket.

"I got something from my secret pal, too," Jake said.

"What?" Tommy asked before he remembered that he was Jake's secret pal.

"Oh, something," Jake said.

Tommy raised his eyebrows. He hadn't gotten Jake anything yet!

"Well, I better go." Jake hurried back to his desk.

At the end of recess, Tommy's class lined up outside Mrs. Hall's door.

"I got a rainbow-colored notepad from my secret pal." April's curls looked like fat brown sausages and bounced when she spoke. "What did you get?" she asked Elizabeth.

"Eraser tops," Elizabeth said. "They're shaped like animals."

"I got markers," said Crystal.

"I didn't get anything," said Jennifer. Sighing loudly, she popped a cherry cough drop into her mouth. She ate cough drops like they were candy.

Tommy pulled his balloon out of his

pocket. He felt guilty when he remembered how Jake had liked it. He should
have gotten Jake something.

Tommy showed April and Jennifer his
balloon.

"Nice," April said.

"I wish I had a balloon like that," said
Jennifer.

Crystal held out her hand. "Can I see
it?"

Tommy handed Crystal the balloon.

After looking at it, Crystal passed Tommy's balloon to Elizabeth. Elizabeth passed it to Mark. Mark passed it to Kyle. By the time Mrs. Hall opened the door to let the kids back into the classroom, Tommy didn't know where his balloon was. His chest felt tight. He slipped out of line to wait beside the door as his class filed in, hoping someone would hand the balloon back.

No one did.

Tommy stayed outside to search for his balloon. He even poked through some bushes at the edge of the playground. But it wasn't anywhere. Could someone have taken it?

Tommy went back inside the classroom. He thought about telling Mrs. Hall his balloon was missing. But they weren't supposed to take toys outside at recess. Balloons weren't exactly toys, were they? Tommy sighed. Mrs. Hall probably thought they were.

"Excuse me," Tommy apologized to Jennifer as he squeezed between their desks. He bumped the crayon box on top of Jennifer's desk. She jumped as the box fell over. Her crayons spilled onto the floor.

"Sorry," Tommy mumbled. He stooped and began picking them up.

"It's okay," Jennifer said. "I was finished coloring."

"Want me to put them inside your desk?" Tommy asked.

"That's all right," Jennifer said quickly, taking the box from Tommy. "I'll do it."

At lunchtime Tommy ate two bites of his tuna sandwich, then stuffed the sandwich back in his sack. He just didn't feel like eating. Not after losing his balloon. Tommy turned to Jennifer. "Do you want my licorice?" he asked, holding up two red sticks.

"Thanks," she said, taking the licorice. "I didn't have a very big lunch today. I thought my mom put some potato chips in my lunch, but they're not in my bag."

"I'm missing something, too," Tommy said. "My balloon." His shoulders slumped. "Everyone was passing it around at recess, and I never got it back."

"Maybe someone dropped it outside," Jennifer suggested.

Tommy shook his head. "I checked."

Jennifer looked down at her desk. "I'm really sorry." She sounded like she felt almost as bad as him. Somehow that made Tommy feel worse.

4

Elizabeth's Fan

The next morning at school, Tommy slipped a package of peppermint gum into Jake's desk before Jake came into the classroom.

"We have a special guest today," Mrs. Hall announced after the bell rang. A darkhaired woman stood next to Tommy's teacher. The woman was so short she only came up to Mrs. Hall's shoulder.

"This is Mrs. Watanabe, Elizabeth's mother," said Mrs. Hall. "Elizabeth asked her to come share her slides of Japan today."

Mrs. Watanabe clicked on the slide projector. The first picture showed an airplane. Red letters on the side of the plane said Japan Airlines. "This was our first trip to Japan," Mrs. Watanabe said. "So it was a very special trip."

"Did you go?" Tommy heard Jennifer ask Elizabeth.

Mrs. Watanabe must have heard, too. She smiled. "Elizabeth stayed with her grandmother while her father and I were gone," she said.

When the slide show was over, Mrs. Hall pointed to a crowded display table at the back of the room. "Mrs. Watanabe brought some things from Japan for us to look at," she said. "Please be careful with them."

The class gathered around the table. Tommy picked up a paper fan. With his finger, he traced the cherry blossoms painted on it.

"Mom and Dad brought that fan back for me," Elizabeth told him. "It folds up really small."

"Cool," Tommy said.

Elizabeth smiled, and moved away.

Tommy closed the fan into its metal frame. Then he opened it again. But this time one of the paper folds caught on the frame, and the fan tore.

Tommy sucked in his breath. He stole a
look at Elizabeth. She was showing April a
kid-sized kimono. Her mother stood in a
corner, talking to Mrs. Hall. Nobody was
paying any attention to him. No one knew
he'd torn the fan.

Maybe he could fix it. Tommy studied
the fan. There was no way he could glue it,
like he had the turtle. And if he taped it,
the tape would pull away the next time the
fan was opened.

Quickly, Tommy folded the fan so the tear didn't show. He shoved the fan under some postcards, hoping no one else would find it.

* * *

After lunch Tommy found a little round tin in his pencil box. "You light up my life, Valentine," read the note under the tin.

Tommy pulled off the lid. The inside was filled with wax. It was a candle!

"That's pretty," Elizabeth said. She giggled. "Your secret pal must like you a lot."

Tommy gulped. She wouldn't giggle like that if she knew he had torn her fan.

Tommy set the candle on top of his desk and took out a pencil for math. Then he searched around in his school box till he found his special shark's head sharpener. He twisted the pencil in its pointy-toothed jaws.

"Cool sharpener."

Tommy looked up. Jake stood over him,

chomping on a piece of gum. Why couldn't he stay at his own desk?

Jake reached for the sharpener. "Can I look at it?"

Tommy handed it to him, even though he didn't want to.

Jake poked his finger in the shark's mouth. "Attack, attack!" he yelled. "It smells my blood!"

Finally Jake gave the sharpener back. Tommy dropped it into his pencil box.

Jake watched. "Did your secret pal give it to you?" he asked.

"No, I've had it since kindergarten," Tommy said.

"Lucky," said Jake.

"I guess so," Tommy said. He'd never thought of himself as lucky before, but the shark sharpener was pretty special. He'd find something for Jake that would be special, too.

5

Pencils for Jake

Tommy leaned close to his desk and took one last look at the three pencils he'd bought for Jake last night.

One was dark blue with silver stars. Another was yellow with black stripes. Like a bumblebee. The third was white. It had red racing cars all over it. Tommy almost wished he could keep the pencils for himself.

Tommy glanced back at Jake's empty desk. Jake was in the reading lab. He'd be out of the room for several more minutes. Now was the perfect time to sharpen the pencils and slip them into Jake's desk.

Jake could sharpen the pencils himself, of course, but Tommy had seen Jake sharpen pencils before. By the time he finished grinding one up, there was hardly anything left but the eraser.

Tommy opened his pencil box to take out his shark sharpener. But where was it? He poked through crayons and pencils and shoved his ruler and glue to one side. The sharpener wasn't there.

Tommy kneeled on the floor and peered inside his desk. He pulled out his journal, his homework folder, his math book, and a wad of papers.

Mrs. Hall looked up from the reading

table, where she sat with a group of kids. She held a finger to her lips, but then she smiled. She probably thought he was cleaning out his desk.

"Where is it?" Tommy muttered more loudly than he'd meant to.

Jennifer coughed, but she didn't say anything. Maybe she hadn't heard him.

"What are you looking for?" Elizabeth asked.

"My pencil sharpener," Tommy said.

"The one that looks like a shark?"

Tommy nodded.

"I'll help you look for it."

While Elizabeth searched the floor around his desk, Tommy reached inside.

He poked his fingers into the dark corners. Nothing.

"It's not on the floor," Elizabeth said.

A lump formed in Tommy's throat. "It's not in my desk, either."

"You can borrow my sharpener." Elizabeth grabbed it out of her desk. "Here."

Tommy took the plain red sharpener Elizabeth held out to him. He didn't really want it, but he didn't want to hurt her feelings. "Thanks." He sharpened Jake's pencils, then handed the sharpener back.

Clutching the pencils, Tommy scraped his chair back and stood. Mrs. Hall looked up from the reading table again. Tommy held up the pencils. "Secret pal gift," he mouthed. Mrs. Hall nodded.

Tommy slipped behind Jake's desk. Reaching inside, he pulled out Jake's school box. Inside was a jumble of empty potato-chip bags. Jake sure must eat a lot of chips.

Suddenly a picture flashed through

Tommy's mind. That day at the coatracks when he'd fixed Elizabeth's turtle Jake had shoved something behind a coat. Something that rustled. Was Jake going to the back of the room to eat potato chips? Why would he do that? Unless . . . Tommy sucked in his breath. Jennifer's missing potato-chip bag! She thought her mom had just left them out of her lunch, but what if . . . ?

No, thought Tommy, Jake wouldn't steal. And yet, Jennifer's potato chips weren't the only things missing.

His heart beating fast, Tommy pushed away the potato-chip bags. He pawed through broken crayons and stubby pencils, but his pencil sharpener wasn't in Jake's box. Neither was his balloon.

The bell rang. Jake would be back any minute! Tommy threw the pencils he'd bought into Jake's box. He shoved the box inside Jake's desk, then slid into his own seat as Jake burst into the room.

6

Jake's Jacket

Tommy watched Jake take off his jeans jacket and hang it over his chair. The jacket was so tight Jake practically had to peel it off.

He found the new pencils right away. "Hey," Tommy heard him say. "Look at these, Jennifer. Pretty cool, huh? Must be from my secret pal." Tommy imagined Jake leaning forward to show Jennifer the pencils.

Jennifer sniffed. "No one gives me anything that nice. I wish I had pencils like those."

Tommy's chest tightened. If he hadn't been in such a hurry he would have kept the pencils. If only he'd had time to search further. Jake must have taken his things. Weren't the potato-chip bags evidence? If the balloon and the sharpener weren't in Jake's desk, they had to be in one of Jake's pockets. Or in Jake's jacket!

Tommy looked back at Jake. He was writing with one of the new pencils. Tommy wished he could snatch it away.

When the recess bell rang Tommy

watched Jake grab a ball and run out the door without his jacket.

Tommy hid behind the coatracks. When he heard the hallway door click shut, he peeked out. Everyone was gone.

Tommy crossed the room. His heart pounded as he laid Jake's jacket on the floor.

Kneeling, he unsnapped a pocket and felt around inside it. Nothing. He checked another pocket. It was empty, too. But in the lower left-hand pocket Tommy's fingers closed on something small and hard.

Biting his lip, Tommy pulled the thing out. His heart fell. It was a key. Probably a house key. Tommy stuffed the key back.

Suddenly, he felt awful. He wouldn't like it if someone searched through his stuff. Tommy glanced at the clock above the blackboard. Only five more minutes till recess was over.

Tommy picked up Jake's jacket. He was about to hang it over the chair when the door clicked open and someone came into the room. Tommy jumped, bumping into Jake's desk so hard Jake's pencil box slid out. Empty potato-chip bags, crayons, and pencils flew everywhere as the box landed upside down on the floor.

7

DISCOVERED!

Elizabeth stared at the mess on the floor. "What are you doing here?" she and Tommy asked at the same time.

"I-I was leaving something for my secret pal," Tommy stuttered. His face felt warm.

Elizabeth knelt beside Tommy. She began picking up crayons and putting them back in the box. "I guess Jake's your secret pal," she said.

Tommy nodded. He reached under Jake's desk to pick up the bumblebee-striped pencil.

Elizabeth picked up the dark blue

pencil with the silver stars. "This is so pretty," she said, running a finger over the stars. "Jake is lucky you're his secret pal."

"Yeah, I guess so." Some pal he was. He'd searched Jake's desk and his jacket and found nothing. But if Jake hadn't taken his things, who else could've done it?

Tommy glanced at the clock. Only one more minute till the bell rang and everyone came back. He threw the last few things into Jake's pencil box and slid the box into Jake's desk.

"Have you bought valentines yet?" Elizabeth asked as they moved away from Jake's desk.

Tommy shook his head.

"They're on sale at the drugstore," Elizabeth said as the bell rung. "I bought some last night. They also have a whole bin of fans." She frowned. "Can you believe it? The one I brought to school yesterday got torn. I wanted to buy a new fan, but I'll have to wait till I get my allowance."

Tommy gulped. How could he tell her he was the one who'd torn it?

At the drugstore that evening, Tommy looked at valentines while his dad searched for toothpaste.

Finally, Tommy chose a box of monster-riddle cards. On one card, a goofy-looking purple dragon asked, "Why do dragons sleep during the day?" The answer was, "Because they hunt knights." Jake might like that one.

Next, Tommy found the bin Elizabeth had told him about. It was next to the checkout counter. The sign read FANS: $1.00 each.

Tommy pulled one out and opened it. Orange flowers were painted on it. Elizabeth would think the flowers were pretty. Tommy closed the fan carefully and set it on the counter along with the valentines. A basket of heart-shaped chocolate lollipops caught his eye. Tommy took out two lollipops—one for Jake and one for Elizabeth.

"Why are you giving me something?" Elizabeth asked Tommy as he handed her the fan and the lollipop the next morning. He'd slipped the other lollipop into Jake's desk. "I thought Jake was your secret pal."

Tommy cleared his throat. "I tore your fan. It was an accident."

Elizabeth's eyes widened. "Oh!"

"I'm sorry," Tommy said.

Elizabeth opened the fan. She traced an orange flower with her finger.

"I wish it could be from Japan," Tommy said. "Like your other one."

Elizabeth peered at the fan closely. Then she pointed to small words at the bottom of the fan.

"Made in Japan," Tommy read.

They laughed.

"This fan is even prettier than my old one," Elizabeth said.

After morning recess, Tommy opened his pencil box and found a package of red licorice and a new sharpener on top of his pencils. The sharpener was shaped like a bulldog. A bulldog with sharp teeth.

Jennifer saw it. She smiled. "Isn't that nice? Now you have a new sharpener."

Hmm. He thought Elizabeth was the only person who knew his old sharpener was gone. But Jennifer would've heard Elizabeth and him talking about it, and seen them searching, too. Now he was

really confused. Could Elizabeth or Jennifer have taken it? Or maybe one of them was his secret pal.

"Hey!" Jake shouted suddenly. Tommy turned to look at him. So did everyone else in the class. Jake's face was red. He pointed to his pencil box. "Somebody took one of my new pencils!"

For a moment, no one said a word. Like the whole class was holding its breath.

Mrs. Hall broke the spell. "Are you sure, Jake?"

"Of course I'm sure! I looked all through my pencil box."

"What does your pencil look like?" Mrs. Hall asked. "We can help you look for it."

Jake calmed down some. "It's blue and it has silver stars on it."

Blue with silver stars? That was the pencil Elizabeth liked so much! This is so pretty, she'd said, running her finger over the stars.

8

Jennifer Gets Sick

But Elizabeth wouldn't take Jake's pencil. She was too nice!

When nobody found Jake's pencil on the floor, Mrs. Hall asked them to search their desks. "Maybe someone picked the pencil up and put it in the wrong desk by mistake," she said.

The pencil didn't turn up.

Tommy stared at Elizabeth out of the corner of his eye. When she left her seat to turn in a homework paper, he pushed back his chair, and tried to peer around her desk to see inside it.

Behind him, Jennifer moaned.

Tommy turned. "What's the matter?" he asked.

Jennifer clutched her stomach. "I feel sick."

She did look kind of pale. "Maybe you should go to the nurse's office," Tommy said. If she really was sick, she might throw up!

Jennifer nodded. Still clutching her stomach, she walked slowly to Mrs. Hall's desk.

Mrs. Hall handed Jennifer a pass to the nurse's office, and Jennifer left.

A moment later, Tommy felt a bump as Jennifer's desk

hit the back of his chair. He turned to see Jake crouched by her desk. Jake grinned, and held up a box of cherry cough drops. "Secret pal gift," he said. "And yesterday I gave her a fancy box of tissues."

Tommy couldn't help grinning, too. But he wondered what Jennifer thought of Jake's gifts. He'd sure be disappointed if that's what his secret pal got him. After all, no one likes to be sick.

"Hey, what's this?" Jake was peering inside Jennifer's desk. He pulled out a wrinkled balloon. It was black with white stars.

Tommy stared. "That's my balloon!"

Tommy and Jake waited with Mrs. Hall as everyone left the room for recess. At last she turned to them.

"I'm glad you came to me about this." She looked them both in the eye. "Thank you for not saying anything to the other children."

Tommy blushed. How could everyone *not* know what was going on? He and Jake hadn't been exactly quiet when they found Tommy's balloon. And his shark sharpener. And Jake's pencil, too.

"Jennifer is still in the nurse's office," Mrs. Hall said. "I'm going to go talk to her. I'm sure she's very sorry for taking your things, and I know she'll want to apologize."

Mrs. Hall frowned a little. "You may take your things, of course. But then I'd like you to put Jennifer's desk back together."

Tommy and Jake nodded.

"What about this?" Tommy asked, picking up the box of cough drops.

Jake shrugged. "I guess she can still have them." He tossed the box into Jennifer's desk.

Tommy felt bad he'd been suspicious of Jake. And Elizabeth, too! His stomach twisted when he thought about how he'd pawed through Jake's things looking for the shark sharpener. He patted his pocket, making sure the sharpener was still safe. He'd make things up to Jake somehow.

The door opened and Mrs. Hall came back into the room. Jennifer followed, her head down. When she looked up, Tommy could see her eyes were red and wet.

Jennifer followed Mrs. Hall to where the

boys were standing. "Go ahead, Jennifer," Mrs. Hall said gently.

Jennifer's chin trembled. Tommy felt sorry for her, remembering how hard it had been to apologize to Elizabeth for tearing her fan.

"I'm sorry I took your things," Jennifer whispered.

"Why did you?" asked Jake. He sounded more curious than angry.

Jennifer's eyes widened. "Everyone else was getting something good from their secret pals. I wanted nice things, too."

Tommy glanced at Jake. He wasn't sure, but it seemed like Jake's face was a little red.

"I'm sorry I took your pencil," Jennifer told Jake.

Then she looked at Tommy. "And I'm sorry I took your balloon and your sharpener." A tear trickled down her cheek. "I hope you don't hate me now."

Mrs. Hall put an arm around Jennifer's

shoulder. "Nobody hates you, Jennifer. You made a mistake. Everybody makes mistakes."

Tommy nodded. He'd sure been mistaken about Jake and Elizabeth.

9

The Party

At last it was Friday. Valentine's Day.

Tommy took his new bulldog sharpener out of his pencil box. It wasn't as nice as his shark sharpener, but it was still pretty cool. It even looked a little ferocious.

Tommy twirled a pencil in his new sharpener. He snarled, and barked softly.

Elizabeth turned around and grinned.

Tommy blushed. She must have heard him.

Mrs. Hall clapped her hands together. "Before we begin our party, you may let your secret pal know who you are," she said with a smile.

Everyone began talking and moving at once.

Before Tommy could get up, Elizabeth leaned toward him. Her eyes sparkled. "I'm glad you like the sharpener I got you, secret pal."

"You?" Tommy said. "You're my secret pal?"

Elizabeth grinned. "I was afraid you'd

guess," she said. "When I came back to the room that day. I didn't know you'd be there. I had to wait till the next morning to slip the licorice into your desk. But that gave me time to buy the sharpener, too."

Tommy smiled. He should have known. "Thanks for all the neat stuff."

"You're welcome." Elizabeth turned away as Crystal tapped her on the shoulder.

Jake was sitting at his desk as Tommy walked toward him. Their eyes met. Before Tommy could change his mind he pulled the shark sharpener out of his pocket. He held it out to Jake. "Happy Valentine's Day, secret pal."

Jake's eyes grew round. "You're giving me your sharpener?"

Tommy nodded.

Jake raised an eyebrow. "Are you sure you don't want to keep it?"

Tommy looked at the sharpener. He

could still change his mind. He looked at
Jake. Jake really wanted the sharpener,
Tommy could tell. He laid the sharpener
on top of Jake's desk. "You keep it."

"Thanks." Jake beamed. "And thanks for
the chocolate lollipop and gum, too. And
the pencils. My mom only buys me plain
ones. She says I use them up too fast."

Tommy grinned.

"Party time!" Mrs. Hall called out.

Jake and Tommy looked at each other. "Food!" they both shouted. They raced to the treats table.

"This is the best part of Valentine's Day," Tommy said, putting two heart-shaped cookies with red sprinkles on a paper plate. He looked over at Jake and laughed. Jake's cheeks puffed out like a chipmunk's. He had already peeled the paper off a pink-frosted cupcake and stuffed half of it into his mouth.

Jake swallowed, then grinned. "I couldn't wait," he said, loading cookies onto his plate. "Sometimes I get so hungry at school I sneak things out of my lunch bag before lunch. My mom wouldn't like it, if she knew. I take two bags of chips when she asks me to make my own lunch."

Tommy nodded. So that was what Jake had been doing at the coatracks. Getting into his own lunch! Jake was big. He probably needed to eat a lot. And to think Tommy used to be scared of him. Just because Jake was big, it didn't make him a bully.

Tommy and Jake passed Jennifer as they grabbed cups of lemonade and headed back to their desks. Jennifer looked up at Jake. "Thanks for the M & M's," she said shyly.

Jake blushed. "Sure."

"M & M's?" asked Tommy as they neared their desks.

Jake shrugged. "Cough drops don't taste as good as candy."

Tommy smiled. Jake was all right.

When the bell rang, Jake stopped by. "Want to sit with me on the bus?" he asked.

"Sure," Tommy said. He crumpled up his paper plate and stuffed it inside his paper cup. Taking aim, he threw the paper cup across the room. Bull's-eye! It landed right smack in the middle of the garbage can.

Jake gave him a thumbs-up. "Nice shot."

Tommy smiled. Together, he and Jake walked out to the bus.

Enjoy More Hyperion Chapter Books!

ALISON'S PUPPY

SPY IN THE SKY

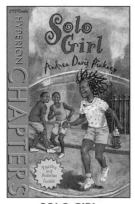

SOLO GIRL

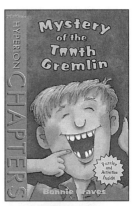

**MYSTERY OF
THE TOOTH GREMLIN**

**MY SISTER
THE SAUSAGE ROLL**

**I HATE MY BEST
FRIEND**

**ALISON'S FIERCE AND
UGLY HALLOWEEN**

SECONDHAND STAR

GRACE THE PIRATE

Hyperion Chapters

2nd Grade
Alison's Fierce and Ugly Halloween
Alison's Puppy
Alison's Wings
The Banana Split from Outer Space
Edwin and Emily
Emily at School
The Peanut Butter Gang
Scaredy Dog
Sweets & Treats: Dessert Poems

2nd/3rd Grade
The Best, Worst Day
Grace's Letter to Lincoln
I Hate My Best Friend
Jenius: The Amazing Guinea Pig
Jennifer, Too
The Missing Fossil Mystery
Mystery of the Tooth Gremlin
No Copycats Allowed!
No Room for Francie
Pony Trouble
Princess Josie's Pets
Secondhand Star
Solo Girl
Spoiled Rotten

3rd Grade
Behind the Couch
Christopher Davis's Best Year Yet
Daughter of Liberty
Eat!
Grace the Pirate
Koi's Python
The Kwanzaa Contest
The Lighthouse Mermaid
Mamá's Birthday Surprise
My Sister the Sausage Roll
Racetrack Robbery
Secret Pal Surprises
Spy in the Sky
Third Grade Bullies